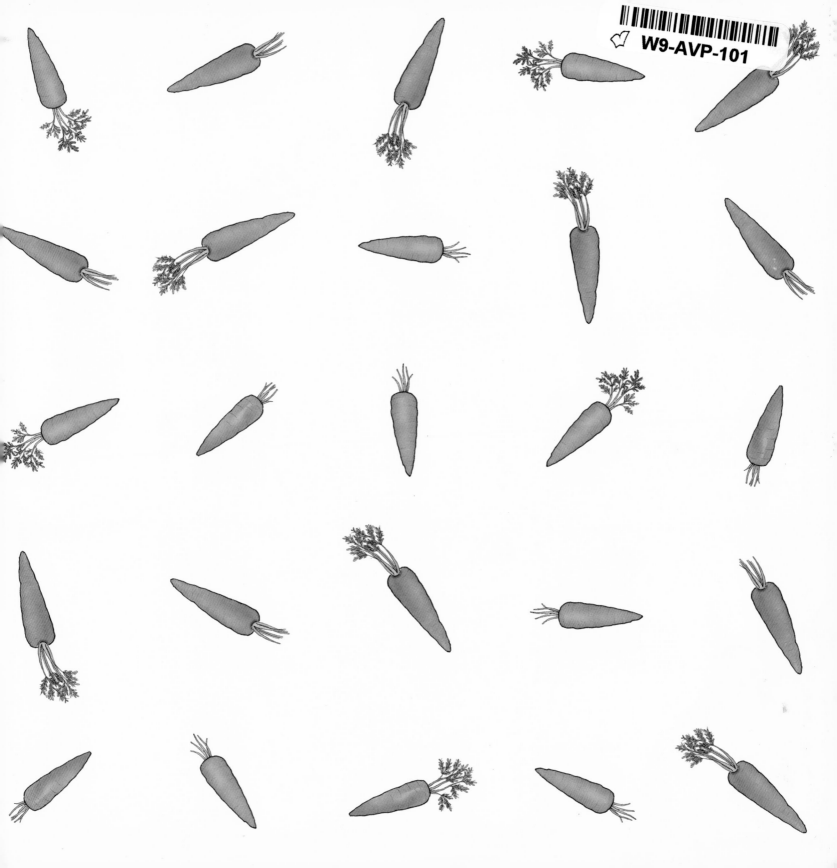

To Dad—for all the wheelbarrow rides

Text and illustration copyright © 2005 by Liane Payne
Design copyright © 2005 by The Templar Company plc

This 2006 edition published by Backpack Books, by arrangement with
The Templar Company plc, Pippbrook Mill, London Road,
Dorking, Surrey, RH4 1JE, UK.

Backpack Books
122 Fifth Avenue
New York, NY 10011

ISBN 0-7607-7185-5

Printed in China

06 07 08 09 MCH 10 9 8 7 6 5 4 3 2 1

Designed by Andy Mansfield
Edited by Sue Harris

a good night bunny book

bunny book

Bunny and the
Great Carrot Race

Liane Payne

BACKPACKBOOKS

NEW YORK

Bunny loved his vegetable patch. Every year he grew lots of tasty things: cabbages in the spring; lettuce in the summer; sprouts in the autumn, and, of course, carrots! Carrots were Bunny's favorite food, and he always grew a handsome crop.

Bunny's Uncle Albert was a prize-winning gardener, too. He lived next door, and was full of useful gardening tips.

"Plant marigolds round your cabbages to keep the slugs away!" he'd say. "And don't forget to dig some compost in before you plant your carrots. Then they'll grow big and juicy!"

Bunny's Auntie May was full of useful advice, too. "Never leave carrots in the ground after the first frost. Bring them to me and I'll make them into a carrot cake for you."

Bunny licked his lips. Aunt May's cakes were so tasty!

One Autumn morning weeks later Bunny woke early. Outside, the sun was shining, but one sniff of the air told him that the first frosts of winter were on their way.

"It's time to harvest my carrot crop," said Bunny, collecting his trusty old wheelbarrow and fork from the shed.

He was just about to start digging when his friend Pippy the Squirrel arrived.

"Oh Bunny, can you help me?" asked
Pippy anxiously. "I need to put my nut
store somewhere safe before winter.
If I could use your wheelbarrow,
it would be done in no time!"
"Of course, Pippy," Bunny said
kindly, and by snack time
the nuts were all safely
stored in a hole in
the old oak tree.

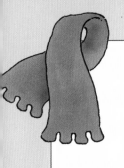

The next day Bunny was up bright and early, determined to catch up on his digging. But it wasn't long before Gus the Mole came calling.

"I'm making a new tunnel for winter, but I'm so cold that I can't dig properly," complained Gus. "Do you think you could help me?"

Now Bunny really wanted to get on with his own digging, but poor Gus looked so miserable he couldn't refuse.

"Of course I'll help," he said, handing Gus his scarf to warm him up.

It took Bunny all day to dig Gus's tunnel, and the next day it was colder than ever. "I must get those carrots up before the ground completely freezes," thought Bunny. But then—disaster struck! The wheel of the barrow hit a stone, and with an almighty crack, off it came. "Now what shall I do?" cried Bunny miserably.

Luckily, help was at hand. "You've helped us!" said Pippy and Gus. "Now, it's our turn to help you!" Uncle Albert took charge and soon everyone was digging up carrots. "We'd best get them into the shed as quick as we can. I think it's going to snow!" he said.

"I know, let's see who can move the biggest pile of carrots," suggested Uncle Albert. "The winner gets a special prize!" And so the Great Carrot Race began! The friends ran up and down Bunny's garden, carrying as many carrots as they could.

In no time all the carrots were safely stored in Bunny's shed. And guess who had moved the biggest pile? Why, Bunny, of course! "And here's your prize!" laughed Auntie May. She had baked the BIGGEST carrot cake Bunny had ever seen! Soon, they were all inside by the fire, munching carrot cake and sipping mugs of hot tea.

Since then, whenever his carrot crop is ready, Bunny always invites his friends round for a Carrot Race, even though Uncle Albert made him a brand new wheelbarrow. Bunny always wins and Auntie May always bakes a carrot cake as his prize.

"It's much more fun than digging up carrots on your own," says Bunny.

"But just as tiring," he adds, as he snuggles
down for a well-earned sleep.
Good night, Bunny!

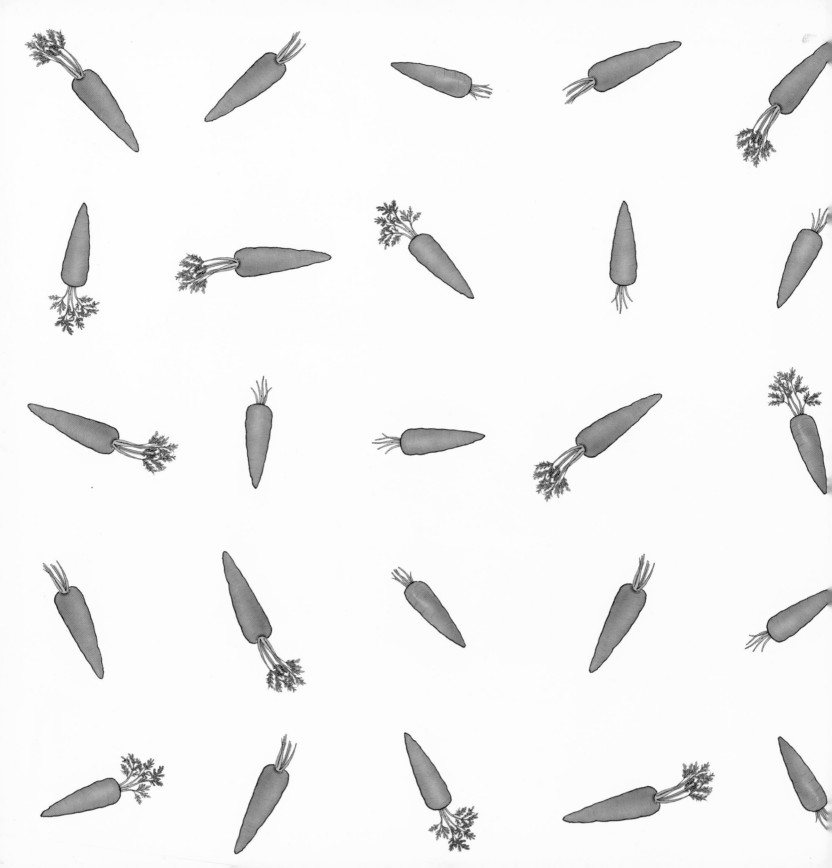